ROTTEN EGGS AND BAD YOLKS

by John Carnell

Illustrated by Anthony Williams

CARNIVAL

Watch out!

Inhu-man is on the loose, causing cruelty to animals wherever he goes.

The mysterious **Big Cheese** has formed a secret team, led by his ex-bodyguard **Aunt Tee**, to combat Inhu-man's evil forces.

Barf
a dog with real muscle

Princess Meow
a reformed alley cat

Polygon
a crazy parrot who can mimic anyone and anything

Neil Shellstrong
the world's first
bionic tortoise

Quickly
Neil's mouse mechanic

Brains
a hyper-intelligent goldfish
from the lost city of Atlantis

By day they live with kind and unsuspecting
RSPCA Inspector Jack, but when danger
threatens they become **The Pet Squad**,
operating from the secret Pet Cave underneath
Jack's cliff-top home.

Just when you thought it was safe
to be cruel to your animals…

Pet Squad Yo!

"What's the matter Jack?" asked Aunt Tee, "Don't you want your boiled egg this morning?"

"No," said Inspector Jack, putting on his coat. "I'm going on a raid tonight and I've got to go and get everything sorted."

He grabbed a piece of toast from the kitchen table and walked to the door. "Besides, those farm fresh eggs haven't been tasting too fresh lately!" Then he said with a grin, "Still, perhaps I can do something about that tonight."

"Umm," thought Aunt Tee, "I wonder what he's up to."

When Jack had gone, Quickly, the mouse mechanic, came into the room. His hands were all covered in grease. "It's done Aunt Tee. Your old banger is fixed."

"Oh goody," she said, "Go and get the others and I'll make some nice cheese sandwiches for our picnic in the country."

"Oh no!" groaned Quickly, "travelling in your old banger I can handle, but cheese sandwiches? Yuk! I hate cheese!"

But in spite of his moans, Quickly was really looking forward to the ride. The Pet Squad were taking a well-earned day off - something they didn't often get the chance to do.

"It's so nice out here," said Barf, as they chugged along the country lanes in Aunt Tee's ancient car. "So peaceful!"

The car backfired, making a loud noise. "Haww! Haww!" squawked Polygon. "It was peaceful until we got here."

He was right. Although Quickly had fixed Aunt Tee's car so that it could run on unleaded petrol, not even his mechanical genius could stop it backfiring. Some things were just impossible.

"Barf's right," said Princess Meow, who was looking around at the countryside. "It's so peaceful out here. And best of all, there's no sign of Inhuman and his foul play!"

Suddenly the car swerved, skidded and went off the road in a blizzard of white feathers. Aunt Tee had narrowly missed a crazy chicken crossing the road. Polygon was tempted to ask why the chicken was crossing the road in the first place, but he thought of a better joke.

"Haww! What was that you said about fowl play? Haw haw!"

It wasn't much better.

They looked at the demented hen as she ran round and round in circles, pecking at the ground. She badly needed help. It looked like this was another job for the Pet Squad.

After a while, they managed to catch the chicken and put her in the car, but even when she calmed down enough to tell them her story, she couldn't stop pecking.

"Peck peck peck! It's horrible in there. Like a prison" she said, pecking at the stuffing hanging out of the back seat. "Peck peck! There are hundreds of us, squashed in row upon row. All we do is peck, peck, lay, lay all day long. I can't take it any more. Those eggs are cracking me up."

The chicken was in a bad way. At last she explained that she used to be a free-range hen who ran free around the farmyard. She used to lay her eggs anywhere she wanted. Then suddenly, overnight, the farmer changed his methods and put all his hens in batteries.

"This smells like Inhu-man's rotten work," said Aunt Tee. "There's only one thing to do - cancel the picnic and check it out."

"Let's go!" yelled the Pet Squad.

The farmer was not happy to see the Pet Squad. "There's nothing wrong with battery farming," he said angrily when Aunt Tee questioned him. "Besides," he scoffed, "they're only dumb birds anyway!"

Polygon got angry and puffed his chest feathers up. "I'll give you dumb birds."

Aunt Tee held Polygon back. "Stay cool, Polygon," she whispered. "I think he's under Inhu-man's spell."

"If I don't put them in batteries," said the farmer, kicking one of the hens, "I'll never make any money from them. Anyway, that's what the chap from the Board of Agriculture said."

It seemed that Inhu-man had been very sly. Posing as an official from the Board of Agriculture, he had hatched his evil plan. He had turned a good farmer bad. What a rotten egg.

"There's only one thing for it!" said Aunt Tee to the Squad. "We'll have to put him under the Pet Lamp!"

The Squad gasped. The Pet Lamp was a special machine invented by Brains. It had the power to remove Inhu-man's evil spells - but only if the victim still had some humanity left.

Aunt Tee got the Pet Lamp from the boot and plugged it into the car battery. The farmer sat down in the back seat, thinking he was being measured up for the nice woolly hat that Aunt Tee said she'd make him.

"Are you sure this is necessary?" asked the farmer, as Aunt Tee placed the device on his head. It had lots of coloured wires coming from it, and the farmer was getting suspicious.

"Here goes," said Brains. He flicked the switch, and a blinding white light shone from the Pet Lamp. The farmer started to shake.

"It's working," said Barf, "Just keep your fingers crossed."

"And your feathers," squawked Polygon, as the farmer opened his mouth - and started talking like Inhuman!

"I'll kill you ALL!" he shouted, " I hate animals. They smell. I hate chickens! Aghhhh!"

Suddenly he stopped shouting and went still. Then he began to stir, as if waking from a deep sleep. "Urr, what happened? Where am I? Are my chickens all right?"

"Phew!" said Aunt Tee, "it worked. He's OK."

After a nice cup of tea the farmer recovered, but he was very angry. "That Inhu-man has got to be taught a lesson," he said, banging his fist on the table. "My poor old chickens have been scared to death. I think it's time he realised who's the head rooster on this farm!"

The Squad cheered.

"Well, guess what?" said Brains. "I happen to know that Inhu-man is coming back here tonight to visit, so why don't we all teach him a lesson!"

"Yeah!" they cried. Then the farmer stopped and looked puzzled as he realised for the first time that he was talking to a bunch of really strange animals. He peered into the fish bowl.

"How did you know that Inhu-man was coming here tonight?" he asked. Brains just swished his tail and smiled. "Let's just say a dickie bird told me!"

They all laughed as they went to the barn. There was a lot to be done.

Meanwhile, not far from the farm, Inspector Jack sat in his van, waiting. "That farmer's for it this time," he thought to himself. "If he's ill-treating those chickens, he's going to get the shock of his life."

The night soon came, and brought with it an evil visitor.

"So," said Inhu-man, snarling at the farmer who was pretending to be under his influence. "Don't you think we could fit a few more chickens into that old shed of yours, eh?"

"Err… er…" stammered the farmer.

"Think of the money," said Inhu-man, rubbing his greasy hands together.

"Well I can't," said the farmer, cowering, "I can't have any more chickens!"

"What!" screamed Inhu-man. "No more chickens?"

"I can't have any more. The Poultry Phantom said that if I do…"

Inhu-man cut him short. "The Poultry Phantom! What on earth are you talking about? Have you gone mad?"

The farmer pretended to be even more frightened than before. "No, I'm not mad. It's real. I thought it was just a local legend. Ever since I was a boy I remember the stories about a giant chicken with red eyes and a dagger beak. People said that it would come at night and peck bad farmers to death!"

Inhu-man started to look worried. "Rubbish! It's a load of rubbish!"

"It's not rubbish," said the farmer, "It's real. It came last night. I heard a noise - a sort of mechanical cluck, cluck, cluck! So I opened the doors and there it was. Huge, white and ghostly! It nearly got me with its beak, but I was too fast for it. Ooh, you should have seen it! Horrible!"

By now, Inhu-man was terrified. He
tried to put on a brave face. He looked
out of the window and saw a strange red
glow coming from the barn. Inhu-man
gulped.

"Have a look if you don't believe me,"
said the farmer, opening the cottage
door. "Or are you too chicken?"

Inhu-man pulled himself together and pushed the farmer aside. "Ha! Scared! Me? No way. It's just a load of old nonsense."

The truth was that Inhu-man had never been more scared in his life. He crept up to the big barn doors. The farmer was right behind him. He listened - but couldn't hear anything. "Ha! Poultry Phantom my aunt!"

Suddenly the barn doors flew open, and there it was. Inhu-man shrieked as he looked into the phantom's fiery eyes. It was just as the farmer had described. It glowed in the darkness of the barn as it flapped its massive wings. Its beak was huge and dagger like, and its claws were metallic and sharply curved. It shrieked back at Inhu-man, sounding like four rusty car horns.

It was too much for Inhu-man to take. He ran, tripped, fell into a pile of manure, got up again, fled, fell into a puddle, scrambled to his feet, bumped into a wall and ran off screaming into the night. The farmer laughed so loud he woke his chickens up. "That's the last I'll ever see of Inhu-man," he chuckled.